Joe Camp's Benji ™

FASTEST DOG IN THE WEST

By Gina Ingoglia
Illustrated by Werner Willis

D1410943

gb GOLDEN PRESS
Western Publishing Company, Inc.
Racine, Wisconsin

0-307-10826-0

Library of Congress Cataloging in Publication Data

Ingoglia, Gina.
    Joe Camp's Benji, fastest dog in the West.

    SUMMARY: Relates how Benji proves his bravery
with a very valiant act of courage and earns his
title "the fastest dog in the west."
    [1. Dogs—Fiction. 2. Rodeos—Fiction]
I. Camp, Joe. II. Willis, Werner. III. Benji.
[Motion picture] IV. Title.
PZ7.I53Jo 1979   [E]   79-10477

As soon as Cindy opened the back door, Benji and Tiffany scampered outside.

"Paul," Cindy called, "it's time for the morning Sweetie-Peetie chase!"

Sweetie-Peetie was sunning herself on Mrs. Finster's fence, waiting for them, as usual. Benji and Tiffany dashed over to her.

"Yeeeoow!" screeched Sweetie-Peetie, and the morning chase was on.

The children, grinning, watched as the animals rushed down the street.

"I'm glad it's sunny for the rodeo today," said Paul.

"I wish the rodeo had a contest for running dogs," said Cindy. "I'll bet that our Benji would be the fastest dog in Silver Creek!"

The animals raced back past the children. Sweetie-Peetie scrambled up the nearest tree. She glared at the two barking dogs, who stood below wagging their tails and panting in the shade.

Mary, the housekeeper, set out a bowl of water. Benji and Tiffany trotted over for a quick drink.

Mrs. Finster called, "Come, Sweetie-Peetie, dear. It's time for your nap."

The pretty white cat clambered down from the tree and scooted home. Mrs. Finster waved. "Good luck at the rodeo, children," she said.

Dr. Chapman strolled into the yard.

"Hi, Daddy," said Paul. "Benji just ran faster than he ever has before!"

Dr. Chapman smiled. "Are you and Cindy ready to do some fancy riding this afternoon?"

"Yes, sir!" laughed Paul. "We've both been practicing very hard for days."

After lunch, they piled into the car. The sun was hot when they arrived at the rodeo grounds. Mary opened the door and let Benji and Tiffany scramble past her.

When everyone was out of the car, Paul looked around. "Where are the dogs?"

"There they are," answered Cindy, pointing her finger, "under that bush."

Mary laughed. "They know where it's cool and shady."

"They'll be all right there," said Dr. Chapman.

But the dogs weren't still for long. They wandered over to a large corral to look at the horses.

"Get along, doggies," said a cowboy. "I'm afraid that you might scare the horses."

Benji and Tiffany scooted off.

They saw a man swinging a rope over his head. It snapped and twirled in loops around him. Benji and Tiffany barked playfully and tried to bite the rope.

"Shoo!" The man laughed. "I'll never be able to practice this way."

The crowd watching the rodeo cheered loudly. Benji and Tiffany ran over to look. They found a small space under a fence, where they could look through and see the arena. It was a perfect spot for watching Paul and Cindy perform.

A calf streaked across the arena. Paul rode after it. He roped the calf, jumped to the ground, and quickly tied the calf's feet together.

Then Paul raised both hands over his head. A cowboy dropped the flag to mark Paul's time. It had taken Paul only fifteen seconds!

Soon Cindy appeared, riding a lively young steer. He whirled and kicked, but Cindy held on tightly.

A horn blared—time was up. The crowd cheered. Cindy had ridden the steer for the whole eight seconds, without being thrown!

A cowboy on a huge Brahma bull shot into the arena. The angry animal bucked and snorted. The cowboy rode well, holding one arm up high. Then, unexpectedly, the cowboy was thrown. He fell head over heels onto the dirt.

A clown came to his rescue. He wore baggy pants with red suspenders, and he waved a broom. The bull began to chase him, while the cowboy ran to safety.

"Oooh, look, a clown!" squealed a little girl. She squeezed past a space in the stands and walked out into the arena. The bull watched her with angry eyes.

"Marnie, come back here!" screamed the little girl's terrified mother.

The frightened clown snatched up the child and started to run. The bull lowered his head and charged after them.

In a flash, Benji was over the fence. Barking wildly, he dashed after the dangerous bull.

"Benji!" cried Paul. "Where did *you* come from?"

The bull heard Benji barking. Now there was someone *new* to chase. He charged after the brave little dog. But he was no match for Benji! Benji darted this way and that way. He dodged here and there, keeping the bull busy until the clown and the little girl were safe.

Then Benji rushed back to the fence. He flipped himself over the top and landed safely next to Tiffany.

Everyone ran over to Benji.

"You ran in the rodeo after all!" exclaimed Cindy. "Now I *know* you're the fastest dog in Silver Creek!"

The cowboy who had ridden the bull smiled. "I've seen a heap of fast movin', but I've never seen anything like that." He tied a first-prize ribbon around Benji's neck.

"Benji," he said with a grin, "*I* know you're the fastest dog in the West!"